Eveline

Includes MLA Style Citations for Scholarly
Secondary Sources, Peer-Reviewed Journal
Articles and Critical Essays

By James Joyce

[Squid Ink Classics Edition]

July 2016

Boston, MA

Eveline

By James Joyce

A Squid Ink Classic

EVELINE

SHE sat at the window watching the evening invade the avenue. Her head was leaned against the window curtains and in her nostrils was the odour of dusty cretonne. She was tired.

Few people passed. The man out of the last house passed on his way home; she heard his footsteps clacking along the concrete pavement and afterwards crunching on the cinder path before the new red houses. One time there used to be a field there in which they used to play every evening with other people's children. Then a man from Belfast bought the field and built houses in it—not like their little brown houses but bright brick houses with shining roofs. The children of the avenue used to play together in that field—the Devines, the Waters, the Dunns, little Keogh the cripple, she and her brothers and sisters. Ernest, however, never played: he was too grown up. Her father used often to hunt them in out of the field with his blackthorn stick; but usually little Keogh used to keep nix and call out when he saw her father coming. Still they seemed to have been rather happy then. Her father was not so bad then; and besides, her mother was alive. That was a long time ago; she and her brothers and sisters were all grown up; her mother was dead. Tizzie Dunn was dead, too, and the Waters had gone back to England. Everything changes. Now she was going to go away like the others, to leave her home.

Home! She looked round the room, reviewing all its familiar objects which she had dusted once a week for so many years, wondering where on earth all the dust came from. Perhaps she would never see again those familiar objects from which she had never dreamed of being divided. And yet during all those years she had never found out the name of the priest whose yellowing photograph hung on the wall above the broken harmonium beside the coloured print of the promises made to Blessed Margaret Mary Alacoque. He had been a school friend of her father. Whenever he showed the photograph to a visitor her father used to pass it with a casual word:

"He is in Melbourne now."

She had consented to go away, to leave her home. Was that wise? She tried to weigh each side of the question. In her home anyway she had shelter and food; she had those whom she had known all her life about her. Of course she had to work hard, both in the house and at business. What would they say of her in the Stores when they found out that she had run away with a fellow? Say she was a fool, perhaps; and her place would be filled up by advertisement. Miss Gavan would be glad. She had always had an edge on her, especially whenever there were people listening.

"Miss Hill, don't you see these ladies are waiting?"

"Look lively, Miss Hill, please."

She would not cry many tears at leaving the Stores.

But in her new home, in a distant unknown country, it would not be like that. Then she would be married—she, Eveline. People would treat her with respect then. She would not be treated as her mother had been. Even now, though she was over nineteen, she sometimes felt herself in danger of her father's violence. She knew it was that that had given her the palpitations. When they were growing up he had never gone for her like he used to go for Harry and Ernest, because she was a girl; but latterly he had begun to threaten her and say what he would do to her only for her dead mother's sake. And now she had nobody to protect her. Ernest was dead and Harry, who was in the church decorating business, was nearly always down somewhere in the country. Besides, the invariable squabble for money on Saturday nights had begun to weary her unspeakably. She always gave her entire wages—seven shillings—and Harry always sent up what he could but the trouble was to get any money from her father. He said she used to squander the money, that she had no head, that he wasn't going to give her his hard-earned money to throw about the streets, and much more, for he was usually fairly bad of a Saturday night. In the end he would give her the money and ask her had she any intention of buying Sunday's dinner. Then she had to rush out as quickly as she could and do her marketing, holding her black leather purse tightly in her hand as she elbowed her way through the crowds and returning home late under her load of provisions. She had hard work to keep the house together and to see that the two young children who had been left to her charge went to school regularly and got their meals regularly. It was hard work—a hard life—but now that she was about to leave it she did not find it a wholly undesirable life.

She was about to explore another life with Frank. Frank was very kind, manly, open-hearted. She was to go away with him by the night-boat to be his wife and to live with him in Buenos Ayres where he had a home waiting for her. How well she remembered the first time she had seen him; he was lodging in a house on the main road where she used to visit. It seemed a few weeks ago. He was standing at the gate, his peaked cap pushed back on his head and his hair tumbled forward over a face of bronze. Then they had come to know each other. He used to meet her outside the Stores every evening and see her home. He took her to see The Bohemian Girl and she felt elated as she sat in an unaccustomed part of the theatre with him. He was awfully fond of music and sang a little. People knew that they were courting and, when he sang about the lass that loves a sailor, she always felt pleasantly confused. He used to call her Poppens out of fun. First of all it had been an excitement for her to have a fellow and then she had begun to like him. He had tales of distant countries. He had started as a deck boy at a pound a month on a ship of the Allan Line going out to Canada. He told her the names of the ships he had been on and the names of the different services. He had sailed through the Straits of Magellan and he told her stories of the terrible Patagonians. He had fallen on his feet in Buenos Ayres, he said, and had come over to the old country just for a holiday. Of course, her father had found out the affair and had forbidden her to have anything to say to him.

"I know these sailor chaps," he said.

One day he had quarrelled with Frank and after that she had to meet her lover secretly.

The evening deepened in the avenue. The white of two letters in her lap grew indistinct. One was to Harry; the other was to her father. Ernest had been her favourite but she liked Harry too. Her father was becoming old lately, she noticed; he would miss her. Sometimes he could be very nice. Not long before, when she had been laid up for a day, he had read her out a ghost story and made toast for her at the fire. Another day, when their mother was alive, they had all gone for a picnic to the Hill of Howth. She remembered her father putting on her mother's bonnet to make the children laugh.

Her time was running out but she continued to sit by the window, leaning her head against the window curtain, inhaling the odour of dusty cretonne. Down far in the avenue she could hear a street organ playing. She knew the air. Strange that it should come that very night to remind her of the promise to her mother, her promise to keep the home together as long as she could. She remembered the last night of her mother's illness; she was again in the close dark room at the other side of the hall and outside she heard a melancholy air of Italy. The organ-player had been ordered to go away and given sixpence. She remembered her father strutting back into the sickroom saying:

"Damned Italians! coming over here!"

As she mused the pitiful vision of her mother's life laid its spell on the very quick of her being—that life of commonplace sacrifices closing in final craziness. She trembled as she heard again her mother's voice saying constantly with foolish insistence:

"Derevaun Seraun! Derevaun Seraun!"

She stood up in a sudden impulse of terror. Escape! She must escape! Frank would save her. He would give her life, perhaps love, too. But she wanted to live. Why should she be unhappy? She had a right to happiness. Frank would take her in his arms, fold her in his arms. He would save her.

She stood among the swaying crowd in the station at the North Wall. He held her hand and she knew that he was speaking to her, saying something about the passage over and over again. The station was full of soldiers with brown baggages. Through the wide doors of the sheds she caught a glimpse of the black mass of the boat, lying in beside the quay wall, with illumined portholes. She answered nothing. She felt her cheek pale and cold and, out of a maze of distress, she prayed to God to direct her, to show her what was her duty. The boat blew a long mournful whistle into the mist. If she went, tomorrow she would be on the sea with Frank, steaming towards Buenos Ayres. Their passage had been booked. Could she still draw back after all he had done for her? Her distress awoke a nausea in her body and she kept moving her lips in silent fervent prayer.

A bell clanged upon her heart. She felt him seize her hand:

"Come!"

All the seas of the world tumbled about her heart. He was drawing her into them: he would drown her. She gripped with both hands at the iron railing.

"Come!"

No! No! No! It was impossible. Her hands clutched the iron in frenzy. Amid the seas she sent a cry of anguish!

"Eveline! Evvy!"

He rushed beyond the barrier and called to her to follow. He was shouted at to go on but he still called to her. She set her white face to him, passive, like a helpless animal. Her eyes gave him no sign of love or farewell or recognition.

MLA Style Citations for Scholarly Secondary Sources, Peer-Reviewed Journal Articles and Critical Essays

Albert, Leonard. "Gnomonology: Joyce's" The Sisters"." *James Joyce Quarterly* 27.2 (1990): 353-364.

Anderson, Chester G. *James Joyce,* London: Thames and Hudson, 1967.

"Araby." *Short Stories for Students*. Ed. Kathleen Wilson. Vol. 1. Detroit: Gale, 1997. 1-15. *Gale Virtual Reference Library*. Web.

Avery, Bruce. "Distant Music: Sound and the Dialogics of Satire in" The Dead"." *James Joyce Quarterly* 28.2 (1991): 473-483.

Barisonzi, Judith. "Who Eats Pigs' Cheeks?: Food and Class in" Araby"."*James Joyce Quarterly* 28.2 (1991): 518-519.

Barney, Rick, et al. "Analyzing" Araby" as Story and Discourse: A Summary of the MURGE Project." *James Joyce Quarterly* 18.3 (1981): 237-254.

Barnhisel, Greg. "Critical Essay" for *Short Stories for Students*, Gale Research, 1997.

Bassić, Sonja, "A Book of Many Uncertainties: Joyce's *Dubliners*," in *ReJoycing: New Readings of Dubliners*, University of Kentucky Press, 1998, pp. 13–40.

Billigheimer, Rachel V. "The Living in Joyce's 'The Dead'," in *CLA Journal,* Vol. XXXI, No. 4, June, 1988, pp. 472-83.

Brown, Homer Obed. *James Joyce's Early Fiction*, Archon, 1975.

Bradbury, Malcolm, and James McFarlane, *Modernism: A Guide to European Literature 1890–1930*, Penguin, 1978.

Brendan, PO Hehir. "Structural Symbol in Joyce's" The Dead"." *Twentieth Century Literature* (1957): 3-13.

Bulson, Eric, "Joyce the Modernist," in *The Cambridge Introduction to James Joyce*, Cambridge University Press, 2006, pp. 17–21.

Bulson, Eric,", "Works: *Dubliners*," in *The Cambridge Introduction to James Joyce*, Cambridge University Press, 2006, pp. 35–42.

Burgess, Anthony. *Here Comes Everybody: An Introduction to James Joyce for the Ordinary Reader*, London: Faber and Faber, 1965.

Burke, Kenneth. "Stages in 'The Dead'." In *Dubliners: Text and Criticism*, Robert Scholes and A. Walton Litz, editors, New York: Penguin, 1996, pp. 395-401.

Chaudhry-Fryer, Mamta. "Power Play: Games in Joyce's *Dubliners*," in *Studies in Short Fiction*, Vol. 32, No. 3, Summer 1995, pp. 319–27.

Collins, Ben L. "Joyce's" Araby" and the" Extended Simile"." *James Joyce Quarterly* 4.2 (1967): 84-90.

Deane, Paul. "Motion Picture Techniques in James Joyce's" The Dead"."*James Joyce Quarterly* 6.3 (1969): 231-236.

Dettmar, Kevin J. H., "James Joyce," in *Dictionary of Literary Biography*, Vol. 162, *British Short-Fiction Writers, 1915–1945*, edited by John H. Rogers, Gale Research, 1996, pp. 160–81.

Dilworth, Thomas. "Sex and Politics in" The Dead"." *James Joyce Quarterly*23.2 (1986): 157-171.

Dilworth, Thomas, "Not 'Too Much Noise': Joyce's 'The Sisters,'" in *Twentieth Century Literature*, Vol. 39, No. 1, Spring 1993, p. 99.

Doherty, Gerald, "The Art of Confessing: Silence and Secrecy in James Joyce's 'The Sisters,'" in *James JoyceQuarterly*, Vol. 35, No. 4, Summer 1998, pp. 657–64.

Doloff, Steven. "On the Road with Loyola: St. Ignatius' Pilgrimage as Model for James Joyce's" Araby"." *James Joyce Quarterly* 28.2 (1991): 515-517.

Doloff, Steven. "Aspects of Milton's Paradise Lost in James Joyce's" Araby"." *James Joyce Quarterly* 33.1 (1995): 113-115.

Doloff, Steven. "Rousseau and the Confessions of" Araby"." *James Joyce Quarterly* 33.2 (1996): 255-258.

Dunleavy, Janet Egleson. "The Ectoplasmic Truthtellers of" The Dead"."*James Joyce Quarterly* 21.4 (1984): 307-319.

Ehrlich, Heyward. "" Araby" in Context: The" Splendid Bazaar," Irish Orientalism, and James Clarence Mangan." *James Joyce Quarterly* 35.2/3 (1998): 309-331.

Ellmann, Richard. "The Backgrounds of 'The Dead'." In *Dubliners: Text and Criticism,* Robert Scholes and A. Walton Litz, editors, New York: Penguin, 1996, pp. 373-88.

Ellman, Richard, *James Joyce,* Oxford University Press, 1983.

"**Eveline**." *Short Stories for Students*. Ed. Ira Mark Milne. Vol. 19. Detroit: Gale, 2004. 58-81. *Gale Virtual Reference Library*. Web.

Feshbach, Sidney. "Fallen on His Feet in Buenos Ayres"(D 39): Frank in" **Eveline**." *James Joyce Quarterly* 20.2 (1983): 223-227.

Fletcher, John. "Joyce, Beckett, and the Short Story in Ireland," in *Re: Joyce'n Beckett*, edited by Phyllis Carey and Ed Jewinski, Fordham University Press, 1992, pp. 20–30.

Florio, Joseph. "Joyce's '**Eveline**,'" in *Explicator,* Vol. 51, No. 3, Spring 1993, pp. 181–84.

Freimarck, John. "'Araby': A Quest for Meaning," in *James Joyce Quarterly*, Vol. 7, no. 4, Summer, 1970, pp. 366-8.

Friedrich, Gerhard. "The Perspective of Joyce's Dubliners." *College English*26.6 (1965): 421-426.

Friedrich, Gerhard, and Florence L. Walzl. "Joyce's Pattern of Paralysis in Dubliners." *College English* 22.7 (1961): 519-520.

Friedrich, Gerhard. "The Gnomonic Clue to James Joyce's Dubliners."*Modern Language Notes* 72.6 (1957): 421-424. Freimarck, John. "" Araby": A Quest for Meaning." *James Joyce Quarterly*7.4 (1970): 366-368.

Gall, Timothy, L., and Susan Bevan Gall, "Ireland," in *Worldmark Encyclopedia of the Nations*, Gale, Cengage Learning, 2009.

Garrett, Roland. "Six Theories in the Bedroom of 'The Dead'," in *Philosophy and Literature,* Vol. 16, No. 1, April, 1992, pp. 115-27.

Garrett, Peter K., ed., *Twentieth Century Interpretations of "Dubliners": A Collection of Critical Essays,* Englewood Cliffs: Prentice Hall, 1968.

Ghiselin, Brewster, "The Unity of Joyce's *Dubliners,"* in *Accent,* Spring 1956, pp. 75–87.

Gibson, Andrew, and Declan Kiberd, *James Joyce*, Reaktion Books, 2006.

Gifford, Don. *Joyce Annotated,* University of California Press, 1982.

Gould, Gerald. A review of *Dubliners. New Statesman,* June 27, 1914, pp. 374-75.

Harry Stone, "'Araby' and the Writings of James Joyce," in *The Antioch Review*, *Vol. XXV. no*. 3, Fall, 1965, pp. 375–445.

Haughey, Jim. "Joyce and Trevor's Dubliners: the legacy of colonialism." *Studies in Short Fiction* 32.3 (1995): 355+. *Literature Resource Center*. Web.

Henigan, Julie. "The Old Irish Tonality": Folksong as Emotional Catalyst in" The Dead." *New Hibernia Review/Iris Éireannach Nua* 11.4 (2007): 136-148.

Ingersoll, Earl G., *Engendered Trope in Joyce's "Dubliners,"* Southern Illinois University Press, 1996.

Ingersoll, Earl G. "The Gender of Travel in" The Dead"." *James Joyce Quarterly* 30.1 (1992): 41-50.

Ingersoll, Earl G. "The Stigma of Femininity in James Joyce's '**Eveline**' and 'The Boarding House,'" in*Studies in Short Fiction,* Vol. 30, No. 4, Fall 1993, pp. 501–10.

Ellen Carol, and Katherine Mullin. "James Joyce, v and Social Purity." (2006): 162-166.

Joyce, James, *James Joyce's "Dubliners": An Illustrated Edition with Annotations,* edited by Bernard McGinley and John W. Jackson, St. Martin's Press, 1993.

Joyce, James, "The Sisters," in *Dubliners*, Tutis Digital Publishing, 2008, pp. 1–8.

LeBlanc, Jim. "All Work, No Play: The Refusal of Freedom in" Araby"."*James Joyce Quarterly* 37.1/2 (1999): 229-233.

Leonard, Garry M., *Reading "Dubliners" Again,* Syracuse University Press, 1993, pp. 95–112.

Leonard, Garry. "Joyce and Lacan:'The Woman'as a Symptom of'Masculinity'in" The Dead"." *James Joyce Quarterly* 28.2 (1991): 451-472.

Levin, Harry. *James Joyce*, New Directions, 1960.

Loe, Thomas. "" The Dead" as Novella." *James Joyce Quarterly* 28.2 (1991): 485-497.

Loomis, C. C. "Structure and Sympathy in Joyce's" The Dead"." *Publications of the Modern Language Association of America* (1960): 149-151.

Luft, Joanna. "Reader Awareness: Form and Ambiguity in James Joyce's" **Eveline**"." *The Canadian Journal of Irish Studies* (2009): 48-51.

Macy, John. *The Critical Game,* New York: Boni and Liveright, 1922, pp. 317-22.

Mandel, Jerome. "The Structure of" Araby"." *Modern Language Studies*(1985): 48-54.

Mandel, Jerome. "Medieval Romance and the Structure of" Araby"." *James Joyce Quarterly* 13.2 (1976): 234-237.

McDermott, John V., "Joyce's 'The Sisters,'" in *Explicator*, Vol. 51, No. 4, Summer 1993, p. 236.

Melzer, Sondra. "In the Beginning There Was" **Eveline**"." *James Joyce Quarterly* 16.4 (1979): 479-485.

Monterrey, Tomás. "Framed Images as Counterpoints in
nes Joyce's' The Dead'/Imágenes enmarcadas como
apuntos en'Los Muertos', de James
" *Atlantis* (2011): 61-74.

n

Morrissey, L.J. "Inner and Outer Perceptions in Joyce's 'The Dead'," in *Studies in Short Fiction,* Vol. 25, No. 1, Winter, 1988, pp. 21-29.

Morse, Donald E. "Sing Three Songs of Araby": Theme and Allusion in Joyce's" Araby." *College Literature* 5.2 (1978): 125-132.

Mosher, Harold F., ed., *ReJoycing: New Readings of "Dubliners,"* University Press of Kentucky, 1998.

Mullin, Katherine. "Don't cry for me, Argentina: **'Eveline'** and the seductions of emigration propaganda." *Semicolonial Joyce* 172 (2000).

Murphy, Terence Patrick. "Interpreting marked order narration: The case of James Joyce's **"Eveline".**" *Journal of literary semantics* 34.2 (2005): 107-124.

Nilsen, Kenneth. "Down among the Dead: Elements of Irish Language and Mythology in James Joyce's" Dubliners"." *The Canadian Journal of Irish Studies* (1986): 23-34.

O'Brien, Eugene. "'Because She Was a Girl': Gender Identity and the Postcolonial in James Joyce's '**Eveline**'." *Studies: An Irish Quarterly Review*93.370 (2004): 201-215.

O'Halloran, Kieran. "The subconscious in James Joyce's '**Eveline**': a corpus stylistic analysis that chews on theFish hook'." *Language and Literature* 16.3 (2007): 227-244.

Ochoa, Peggy. "Joyce's" Nausicaa": The Paradox of Advertising Narcissism." *James Joyce Quarterly* 30 (1993): 783-793.

Osteen, Mark. "Dubliners." *Studies in Short Fiction* 32.3 (1995): 483B+. *Literature Resource Center*. Web.

Owens, Cóilín. "The Mystique of the West in Joyce's" The Dead"." *Irish University Review* 22.1 (1992): 80-91.

Pecora, Vincent P. "" The Dead" and the Generosity of the Word."*Publications of the Modern Language Association of America* (1986): 233-245.

Pindar, Ian, *James Joyce*, Haus Publishing, 2005.

Pound, Ezra. *"Dubliners* and Mr. James Joyce," in *Egoist*, Vol. 1, No. 14, July 15, 1914, p. 267.

Pound, Ezra. *"Dubliners* and Mr. Joyce." In *James Joyce: The Critical Tradition*, Robert H. Deming, editor, New York: Barnes and Noble, 1970, pp. 66-68.

Rapp, Eric. Overview of "The Dead," for *Short Stories for Students*, The Gale Group, 1999.

Rice, Thomas Jackson. "Dante... Browning. Gabriel.. Joyce: Allusion and Structure in" The Dead"." *James Joyce Quarterly* 30.1 (1992): 29-40.

Rice, Thomas Jackson. "Paradigm lost: 'Grace' and the arrangement of 'Dubliners.'(Special 'Dubliners' Number)." *Studies in Short Fiction* 32.3 (1995): 405+. *Literature Resource Center*. Web.

Riquelme, John Paul. "Joyce's" The Dead": The Dissolution of the Self and the Police." *Style* (1991): 488-505.

Roberts, Robert P. "" Araby" and the Palimpsest of Criticism or, through a Glass Eye Darkly." *The Antioch Review* 26.4 (1966): 469-489.

Roberts, R. P. "The Palimpsest of Criticism; or, Through a Glass Eye Darkly," in *The Antioch Review*, Vol. XXVI, 1966-67, pp. 469-89.

Robinson, David W. "The Narration of Reading in Joyce's" The Sisters"" An Encounter," and" Araby"." *Texas studies in literature and language* 29.4 (1987): 377-396.

Russell, Richard Rankin, and KATHERINE MULLIN. "James Joyce, Sexuality and Social Purity." (2005): 491-493.

Salma, Umme. "Orientalism in James Joyce's "Araby"." *Research on Humanities and Social Sciences* 2.2 (2012): 67-79.

Scholes, Robert. "Semiotic Approaches to a Fictional Text: Joyce's **Eveline**." *James Joyce Quarterly* 16.1/2 (1978): 65-80.

Scholes, Robert and A. Walton Litz, editors. *Dubliners: Text, Criticism, and Notes*, Penguin, 1996.

Stone, Harry. "" Araby" and the Writings of James Joyce." *The Antioch Review* 25.3 (1965): 375-410.

Sultan, Stanley. "Dublin Boy and Man in 'The Sisters,'" in *Joyce and the City: The Significance of Place*, edited by Michael Begnal, Syracuse University Press, 2002, pp. 85–97.

Swartzlander, Susan, "James Joyce's 'The Sisters': Chalices and Umbrellas, Ptolemaic Memphis and Victorian Dublin," in *Studies in Short Fiction*, Vol. 32, No. 3, Summer 1995, p. 295.

Schwarz, Daniel R. "Gabriel Conroy's Psyche: Character as Concept in Joyce's 'The Dead'." In *The Dead,* Daniel R. Schwarz, editor, New York: St. Martin's Press, 1994, pp. 102-24.

Shurgot, Michael W. "Windows of Escape and the Death Wish in Man." *Eire-Ireland,* Vol. 17, No. 4, 1982, pp. 58-71.

Sosnoski, James J. "" Story and Discourse" and the Practice of Literary Criticism:" Araby," a Test Case." *James Joyce Quarterly* 18.3 (1981): 255-265.

Tate, Allen. "The Dead." In *Dubliners: Text and Criticism,* Robert Scholes and A. Walton Litz, editors, New York: Penguin, 1996, pp. 389-94.

Taube, Myron. "Joyce and Shakespeare:" **Eveline**" and" Othello"." *James Joyce Quarterly* 4.2 (1967): 152-154.

"The Dead." *Short Stories for Students*. Ed. Tim Akers. Vol. 6. Detroit: Gale, 1999. 83-113. *Gale Virtual Reference Library*. Web.

"The Sisters." *Short Stories for Students*. Ed. Sara Constantakis. Vol. 32. Detroit: Gale, 2011. 250-272. *Gale Virtual Reference Library*. Web.

Tieger, Leah. Critical Essay on "The Sisters," in *Short Stories for Students*, Gale, Cengage Learning, 2011.

Times Literary Supplement. A review of *Dubliners,* June 18, 1914, p. 298.

Torchiana, Donald T. "Joyce's **Eveline** and the Blessed Margaret Mary Alacoque." *James Joyce Quarterly* 6.1 (1968): 22-28.

Torchiana, Donald T. "The Ending of" The Dead": I Follow Saint Patrick."*James Joyce Quarterly* 18.2 (1981): 123-132.

Trudell, Scott. Critical Essay on **"Eveline**," in *Short Stories for Students,* Gale, 2004.

Walzl, Florence L. "The Liturgy of the Epiphany Season and the Epiphanies of Joyce." *Publications of the Modern Language Association of America*(1965): 436-450.

Walzl, Florence L. "Pattern of Paralysis in Joyce's Dubliners: A Study of the Original Framework." *College English* 22.4 (1961): 221-228.

Walzl, Florence L. "Gabriel and Michael: The Conclusion of" The Dead"."*James Joyce Quarterly* 4.1 (1966): 17-31.

Werner, Craig Hansen, *"Dubliners": A Pluralistic World,* Twayne Publishers, 1988, p. 11.

Wheatley-Lovoy, Cynthia D. "The Rebirth of Tragedy: Nietzsche and Narcissus in" A Painful Case" and" The Dead"." *James Joyce Quarterly* 33.2 (1996): 177-193.

Wilson, Edmund, *Axel's Castle,* Macmillan, 1991, p. 192.

Yourgrau, Palle. "The dead." *The Journal of philosophy* 84.2 (1987): 84-101.

50647816R00022

Made in the USA
Middletown, DE
02 November 2017